TITLE:	Crabapple Trouble
CREATOR:	Kaeti Vandorn
IMPRINT:	Random House Graphic
PUBLICATION DATE:	August 11, 2020
HC ISBN:	978-1-9848-9680-3
HC TENTATIVE PRICE:	$12.99 US/$17.99 CAN.
GLB ISBN:	978-0-593-12526-7
GLB TENTATIVE PRICE:	$15.99 US/$21.99 CAN.
EBOOK ISBN:	978-1-9848-9681-0
PAGES:	176
TRIM SIZE:	6-1/2" x 8-1/2"
COLOR:	FULL COLOR
AGES:	5–8

Please send any review or mention of this book to:
Random House Children's Books Publicity Department
1745 Broadway, Mail Drop 9-1
New York, NY 10019
rhkidspublicity@penguinrandomhouse.com

Dear Readers,

This season of books is all about you.

Each new season of books from Random House Graphic is all about you, actually.

We want everyone to have a graphic novel they love—a book that speaks to them and what they're interested in reading about, whether it's magic or vegetables or family or music. And with each season and every new book, we're building an imprint with more and more voices and more and more stories.

So that everyone can have a graphic novel just for them.

When I was a kid, the only comics-format stories I had access to were the ones in the newspapers. Today, I'm delighted that comics have come out of those three- and four-panel strips to a space on our bookshelves, with work that ranges from silly and fun to thoughtful and complicated. So I can have all the kinds of graphic novels I want to read—and so can you.

And we're building your library with new graphic novels every season here at Random House Graphic.

Happy reading!

Gina Gagliano
Publishing Director

CRABAPPLE TROUBLE

Kaeti Vandorn

Visit us on the Web! RHKidsGraphic.com • @RHKidsGraphic

Educators and librarians, for a variety of teaching tools, visit us at RHTeachersLibrarians.com

Library of Congress Cataloging-in-Publication Data
Names: Vandorn, Kaeti, author, artist.
Title: Crabapple trouble / Kaeti Vandorn.
Description: First edition. | New York : RH Graphic, [2020] | Audience: Ages 5–7 | Audience: Grades 2–3 |
Summary: "Callaway just wants to help her friends but the pressure of an
upcoming contest is giving her anxiety"—Provided by publisher.
Identifiers: LCCN 2019026171 | ISBN 978-1-9848-9680-3 (hardcover)
ISBN 978-0-593-12526-7 (library binding) | ISBN 978-1-9848-9681-0 (ebook)
Subjects: LCSH: Graphic novels. | CYAC: Graphic novels. | Contests—Fiction. |
Friendship—Fiction. | Anxiety—Fiction.
Classification: LCC PZ7.7.V24 Cr 2020 | DDC 741.5/973—dc23

Designed by Patrick Crotty

MANUFACTURED IN CHINA
10 9 8 7 6 5 4 3 2 1
First American Edition

A comic on every bookshelf.

CRABAPPLE TROUBLE

Kaeti Vandorn

HA
HA
HA
HA
WOOP!
YAH!

IT'S FINALLY HERE!
WHAT IS IT?
COME TAKE A LOOK, EVERYONE!
I SAW THEM PUT IT UP YESTERDAY!

IT'S A POSTER FOR THE SUMMERTIME FAIR!

THERE'S A PRODUCE COMPETITION! SOUNDS FUN!
Summertime fair
Call for ENTRIES
Produce Competition
Presented by
the Forest Fairy Kingdom
Fairy prizes Galore
Contest Dates
THE ENTRY DATE IS COMING UP SOON. ONLY TWO WEEKS FROM TODAY!
I'VE WAITED ALL YEAR FOR THIS!
THAT SOON? IS THERE ENOUGH TIME TO PREPARE?
Doggo
Day
Takeo
I'LL JUST LOOK AT IT LATER...
OH! CALLAWAY!
DID YOU HEAR ABOUT THE COMPETITION?
YOU'LL ENTER SOMETHING TOO, WON'T YOU?

OF COURSE SHE WILL, CLEMENTINE!

THE WHOLE ORCHARD IS PITCHING IN.

WE'RE MAKING DECORATIVE BASKETS!

AND PRESERVES!
HA
TEE
HEE
HA
HA
HA

WHAT GOOD IDEAS YOU ALL HAVE!

YES, WELL, UM.
I SUPPOSE I'LL THINK OF S-SOMETHING.
ULP!

DID YOU SEE THAT THE WINNERS GET FAIRY PRIZES?!
WHAT COULD THOSE BE?
OH OH
BACK TO WORK I GO!
YEAH, ME TOO.

PRIZES!
GOODBYE, CALLA!
I CAN'T WAIT TO SEE EVERYONE'S STUFF!
YEAH!

GULP

CHAPTER 1

SEE THIS PEACH?

IT'S THE BEST I'VE GROWN!
I'LL WIN A PRIZE WITH IT FOR SURE!

IT'S SO BEAUTIFUL, PEACHY!
MY FRUIT TURNED OUT BIG THIS YEAR, TOO. EVERYONE'S DID!
HUH! WAS IT SOMETHING IN THE COMPOST?

WHY DID I LET THEM TALK ME INTO THIS!
WHAT A BAD IDEA. STUPID, STUPID!

PEACHY'S FRUIT IS MUCH BIGGER THAN MINE.
I KNOW CRABAPPLES ARE SMALL, ANYWAY.
IT'S PART OF WHAT MAKES THEM SPECIAL.

BUT MY FRIENDS ARE SO QUICK TO NOTICE DIFFERENCES!
THEY'RE SURE TO SEE MY APPLES ARE SMALL AS EVER THIS YEAR.

WH-WHAT IF THEY THINK IT'S MY FAULT MY APPLES ARE SMALL?
WHAT IF THEY'RE RIGHT? WHAT IF I DID SOMETHING WRONG?
WHAT AM I GOING TO DO! WHAT WILL I SAY???

POP

OOF!
BONK
BUMP
ACK!

OW!
BAP

FWOOOP!

AAAAAAAA

Z z z

OW!

A A A A AAAAAAAA

FOO OMP

HNGHH

GOODNESS GRACIOUS!

WOULD YOU CALL THIS NORMAL, MISS? ARE YOU ALL RIGHT?
IT'S NOT EVERY DAY YOU SEE A FLYING HEAD!

THIS ISN'T NORMAL AT ALL!
THIS HAS NEVER HAPPENED TO ME BEFORE!

OH MY!

SHE ROLLED FROM ALL THE WAY UP THERE?
THAT'S QUITE THE TUMBLE.

YOU'RE ONE OF THOSE KIDS FROM THE ORCHARD! WHAT'S YOUR NAME?
I'M CALLAWAY. CAN YOU FIX ME, MR. FAIRY?

I'M THISTLE! I'LL HELP YOU OUT, CALLAWAY.
NOTHING TO IT!

LET'S SEE WHERE YOUR BODY IS HIDING.

IS IT UNDER HERE?

HOW ABOUT OVER HERE?

HERE'S SOME GOOD NEWS.
IT WILL BE EASIER FOR YOU TO WIN AT BALL GAMES THIS WAY!

HA HA HA H
HA HA

THAT'S GOOD! YOUR GIGGLES AREN'T BROKEN!

I SAW YOUR BODY UP THE HILL.
SHOULD WE GO FIND THE REST OF YOU?

WOOOOMP

THAT SAVES US SOME TROUBLE!
BACK TOGETHER YOU GO.

NO BUMPS OR SCRAPES?
LOOKING GOOD!
AND YOUR BALANCE SEEMS ALL RIGHT?
HUP
HUP
HUP

PHEW!
IT FEELS NICE TO BE BACK IN ONE PIECE.

I BET IT DOES. YOU MUST HAVE BEEN REALLY UPSET TO LOSE YOUR HEAD LIKE THAT.

I HEARD WHAT YOU SAID BEFORE, ABOUT YOUR FRIENDS AND YOUR APPLES?
IT SOUNDS LIKE A LOT IS GOING ON.

I'M OKAY NOW!
I JUST, UM, LOST MY BALANCE.

PLOP!

I KNOW HOW YOU FEEL.
MY FRIENDS HAVE DIFFERENT IDEAS THAN I DO ALL THE TIME.
I TRY NOT TO WORRY TOO MUCH.
IT'S NONE OF MY BUSINESS WHAT OTHER PEOPLE SAY OR THINK.

SOMETIMES I CAN'T STOP THINKING ABOUT WHAT OTHER PEOPLE WILL SAY.

NOT WORRYING TAKES PRACTICE, CALLAWAY!
BUT IT'S WORTH THE TROUBLE IF YOU TRY IT!

I SUPPOSE I COULD TRY.

THERE YOU GO. THAT'S A GOOD FIRST STEP.

AWOOOOOOOO

DID YOU HEAR THAT?

AAA WOOOOOOOooo!
AAwoooooo
IT CAME FROM OVER THERE.

AWOOOOO!
TRICKS! TRICKS? HERE TRICKS!

NO ONE HERE? BOO!

THAT'S MY FRIEND BLUEBELL!

HI, BLUEBELL! WHAT ARE YOU UP TO?

IS THAT THISTLE?

IT'S TERRIBLE! HORRIBLE! AWFUL!
I'VE LOST MY FAIRY TRICKS!

I WAS TAKING THEM FOR A WALK JUST NOW...THEY WERE SO WELL BEHAVED!
BUT THEN THEY DECIDED TO PLAY A GAME OF CHASE.

NOW THEY'RE HIDING, AND I CAN'T FIND THEM!

THAT'S TOO BAD...
WOULD YOU LIKE SOME HELP?

WELL, I'VE LOOKED EVERY PLACE I CAN THINK.

BUT I'M NOT SURE I WANT HELP FROM A LAYABOUT LIKE THISTLE.
I REMEMBER WHAT HAPPENED LAST TIME HE LOOKED AFTER MY TRICKS!

ZZZ
WHILE HE WAS NAPPING, THEY CAUSED ALL KINDS OF TROUBLE!

DON'T WORRY, I'M WIDE AWAKE RIGHT NOW.

BUT HOW DO I KNOW YOU WON'T FALL ASLEEP AGAIN?
OR DO SOMETHING KOOKY WHEN I'M NOT LOOKING!!!

EXCUSE ME, BLUEBELL?

I'LL HELP YOU! ONLY I DON'T KNOW WHAT A FAIRY TRICK IS. IS IT SOME KIND OF PET?

THEY'RE THE THINGS WE FAIRIES KEEP FOR MISCHIEF MAGIC.
THEY COME IN ALL SHAPES AND SIZES, AND THEY'RE VERY GOOD AT HIDE-AND-SEEK.

THERE'S AN AWFUL LOT OF PLACES TO HIDE HERE.

DON'T WORRY! I KNOW SOME HIDING PLACES.
HOW BIG ARE THESE TRICKS?

ABOUT THIS BIG!

IF I WERE A TRICK, WHERE WOULD I HIDE?

OH! THERE'S SOMETHING HERE.

YOU FOUND ONE! THAT'S AN ORNERY ONE!

LET'S LOOK BEHIND THE TOOLSHED NEXT!

HERE YOU ARE! SAFE AS CAN BE!

WHAT ABOUT THAT BIRD'S NEST? DO TRICKS LIKE TO HIDE UP HIGH?

I COULD FLY UP AND TAKE A LOOK.

ALL RIGHT, BUT PLEASE BE CAREFUL NOT TO SCARE THEM!

HERE WE ARE! LOOK AT YOU!

THAT'S ALL THE HIDING SPOTS I KNOW DOWN HERE.
LET'S HEAD BACK TO THE ORCHARD AND LOOK.

YOU FOUND ANOTHER! YOU'RE GOOD AT THIS GAME!
DO YOU HAVE ANY MORE IDEAS?

I'M STILL MISSING A FEW MORE.
THEY'VE GOT TO BE AROUND HERE SOMEWHERE.

WHAT ABOUT THOSE BAGS, CALLAWAY?
THEY LOOK COZY.

THAT'S NUMBER FIVE! THERE'S ONLY ONE LEFT NOW!

ONE MORE, HUH?

WHERE ELSE IS THERE TO HIDE?
HIDING IN THE TREES SEEMS TOO EASY!

!

THAT'S THE LAST ONE!

YOU'VE FOUND THEM ALL! THANK YOU SO MUCH!

AW, YOU'RE WELCOME.
IT WASN'T TOO HARD ONCE WE STARTED.

YOU REALLY HELPED ME OUT.
I WOULDN'T HAVE FOUND THEM ALL WITHOUT YOUR HELP!

YOU'RE A VERY CLEVER GIRL, KNOWING SO MANY PLACES TO HIDE.

AND THISTLE TOO?

YES. THISTLE TOO.

ALL RIGHT, TRICKS!
MARCH!
INTO THE WOODS WITH YOU!

YOU TWO LOOK AFTER YOURSELVES, NOW! GOODBYE!

GOODBYE, BLUEBELL!

THIS HAS BEEN FUN, CALLAWAY.
I'M GLAD YOU'RE FEELING BETTER!

I SHOULD FINISH MY NAP BEFORE IT GETS DARK.
GOODBYE, THISTLE. HAVE A NICE NAP!

YAWN

ZZZ Z Z

I DO FEEL BETTER.

TOO BAD IT TOOK ALL DAY!

CHAPTER 2

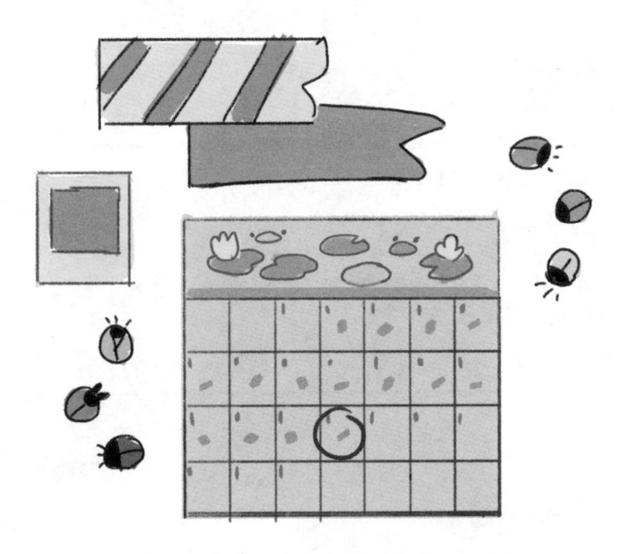

RAIN, RAIN, RAIN.

THE ENTRY DATE FOR THE CONTEST IS TWO WEEKS FROM TODAY.
THAT'S TWO WEEKS TO DECIDE WHAT I'M GOING TO DO.

WHAT TO DO?
MAYBE I COULD COOK SOMETHING?

APPLESAUCE?

APPLE JELLY?

MY APPLES ARE GOOD FOR BAKING, I SUPPOSE...

THEY'RE SUPPOSED TO BE TART AND CRISPY, A LOT LIKE AVI'S PIE CHERRIES!
BUT EVERY APPLE TASTES DIFFERENT, NO MATTER HOW CAREFULLY YOU GROW THEM!

WHAT IF MY APPLES ARE BLAND AND PITHY THIS YEAR?
WHAT IF THEY TASTE AWFUL?

POP

WHOOP

SPROING

AAAAAAAAA

BONK!

OW!

HNGHGHH
WHAT WAS THAT?

AN EARTHQUAKE?

IT'S CALLAWAY!
THISTLE?
IS THAT YOU MAKING EVERYTHING SPIN?

MORE TROUBLE, HUH?
WE'LL SORT THIS OUT.

THANK YOU FOR THE HELP AGAIN.
I'M NOT SURE WHY THIS KEEPS HAPPENING. IT'S SUCH A BOTHER!

YOU WEREN'T WORRYING ABOUT YOUR APPLES AGAIN, WERE YOU?

M-MAYBE A LITTLE BIT.

CALLAWAY, YOU'LL SAVE SOME ENERGY IF YOU GET YOUR WORRIES UNDER CONTROL!
TRY NOT TO THINK SO MUCH ABOUT WHAT MIGHT HAPPEN.

I LIKE TO FOCUS ON WHAT'S HAPPENING NOW.
ARE YOUR FRIENDS REALLY SO TROUBLESOME TO YOU?

NO, IT'S NOTHING LIKE THAT.
IT JUST FEELS BAD TO DISAPPOINT SOMEONE WHEN THEY EXPECT THE BEST FROM YOU!

THAT'S FAIR.
BUT YOU CAN'T WORRY ABOUT PLEASING EVERYONE ALL THE TIME.

I SURE DON'T!

THAT'S HALF THE FUN, NOT KNOWING WHAT PEOPLE WILL SAY TO YOU!
Hmmm.

WHY NOT FIND SOMETHING TO KEEP YOUR MIND OFF THINGS FOR NOW?

THERE'S STILL TWO WEEKS UNTIL THE CONTEST.
YOUR APPLES HAVE PLENTY OF TIME TO RIPEN.

WHAT DO YOU THINK?

OKAY. I CAN TRY.
THAT'S THE SPIRIT!

NOW, HOW ABOUT WE TIDY UP A LITTLE.

HEY, THISTLE? WHAT WERE YOU DOING IN MY DESK DRAWER?

OH!

IT'S A SECRET!
SOMETHING SPECIAL FOR LATER.

THAT REMINDS ME!

COULD I BORROW YOUR SCISSORS, TAPE, AND THIS...ER...
WHATEVER THIS THING IS?

A PAPER PUNCH? YES! PLEASE HELP YOURSELF.

THANKS!
I'LL BE SURE TO PUT THINGS BACK WHEN I'M FINISHED.

NOW, DON'T PAY ATTENTION TO THIS.
IT'S A SECRET, ALL RIGHT?

OKAY.
YAWN.
I KNOW ALL ABOUT KEEPING SECRETS.

GOOD NIGHT, CALLAWAY!
YAWN
GOOD NIGHT, THISTLE.

FIND SOMETHING TO KEEP BUSY, HUH...

CHAPTER 3

TUESDAY

WEDNESDAY
THURSDAY

FRIDAY

MONDAY

IDEAS

THE CONTEST IS NEXT WEEK.

WHAT AM I GOING TO DO?
NOTHING I THINK OF SEEMS GOOD ENOUGH!

NO!
IT'S TIME TO GET THINGS DONE!

HI, CALLAWAY!

OH, CALLAWAY! YOU'RE GOING TO FIX THE BASKETS AGAIN TODAY?
ISN'T THAT NICE?
IT WAS SUPPOSED TO BE MY TURN.

WE'VE BEEN SO BUSY GETTING READY FOR THE CONTEST.
YOU'RE HELPING US OUT SO MUCH!
OF COURSE! YOU KNOW I LOVE HELPING!

DON'T WORK TOO HARD!

THIS IS KEEPING ME BUSY ENOUGH!
I HAVEN'T LOST MY HEAD ONCE SINCE I STARTED ALL THIS WORK!

I'M GLAD TO HEAR THAT!

HI, THISTLE! TAKING A NAP?

YOU SEEM TO BE CALMER TODAY.
ANY IDEAS FOR THE CONTEST?

NOPE. NOT ONE!
BUT YOUR ADVICE TO STAY BUSY HAS HELPED KEEP MY HEAD ON.

THAT'S GREAT, CALLAWAY!

IT'S A START, ANYWAY!

I STLL HAVE TO THINK OF SOMETHING.
MAYBE I CAN USE ONE OF THESE...

THIS BASKET IS CUTE! AND IT'S JUST ABOUT THE RIGHT SIZE.

I'M SURE IT WILL BE LOVELY.

JUST A FEW MORE BLOSSOMS, LILY! AND SOME OF THESE SPECIAL STICKS!

DON'T FORGET THE BERRIES, WILLOW!

PHEW!
OF COURSE! WE NEED LOTS OF THOSE.

AND SOME OF THESE LITTLE THINGS!

OH NO...I DON'T THINK THOSE WILL FIT!

IT CAN'T BE FULL ALREADY!
MAYBE IF I LOOSEN THIS.

PWOF!

NO!
NO!
NO!
HELP!
EEK!

OH DEAR!

DON'T LET IT ROLL AWAY!
QUICK, QUICK! MAKE IT STOP!

NICE CATCH!
PHEW!

OUR INGREDIENTS! YOU SAVED THEM!

WOW, WE REALLY DID COLLECT A LOT!

I TOLD YOU, WILLOW!
WE'VE BEEN COLLECTING FOR DAYS!

BUT WITH OUR BUNDLE BROKEN...
WHAT WILL WE DO? WE'RE ALMOST OUT OF TIME!

I GUESS YOU'LL HAVE TO START OVER AGAIN.

START OVER?!

THISTLE, YOU DON'T UNDERSTAND.
WE HAVE TO FINISH THIS PROJECT TONIGHT!

THERE ISN'T TIME TO GATHER EVERYTHING AGAIN.

SINCE YOU PUT IT THAT WAY! SORRY FOR THE BAD IDEA.

ANY IDEAS, CALLAWAY?

OH!

WHAT IF YOU USE THIS BASKET FOR YOUR COLLECTION? IT HAS ROOM TO SPARE.

THAT COULD WORK.
IT'S BIG ENOUGH, BUT ISN'T IT TOO BIG FOR US TO CARRY?

DON'T WORRY.
I'LL CARRY IT
FOR YOU.

YOU
WILL?!

THAT'S
PERFECT!
WE'LL GET
OUR WORK DONE
FOR SURE.

GOOD WORK, CALLA.
WE'LL GET THESE
TWO SETTLED IN NO
TIME AT ALL!

NOT SO FAST!

WE DON'T NEED YOUR HELP, THISTLE.

IF YOU CAN'T FOLLOW OUR DIRECTIONS...

THERE'S NO TIME FOR SLOPPY WORK.
THIS JOB REQUIRES PRECISION!

OH. I SEE.

I'VE GOT A NAP TO FINISH, ANYWAY!

YAWN!

GOOD LUCK WITH YOUR WORK.
I'LL BE HERE IF YOU NEED ANYTHING.

YOU'RE PICKY ABOUT HELP, HUH?
I GUESS WE ARE.
YUP.

I DO FEEL BAD FOR THISTLE.

HE WANTS TO HELP, BUT HE'S NOT CUT OUT FOR IT.

WE CAN'T TRUST HIM WITH THINGS LIKE THIS. THE WORK IS TOO IMPORTANT.

ENOUGH CHIT CHAT!

FIRST, WE NEED TO ORGANIZE!
THEN WE'LL SEE WHAT WE'RE MISSING!

MOST OF IT IS STILL HERE.
LOOKS LIKE WE'RE ONLY MISSING A FEW THINGS!

JUST SOME BERRIES AND BLOSSOMS LEFT.

AND ONE OF THOSE TWISTY ROOTY THINGS FROM THAT ONE PLANT!

I KNOW JUST THE ONES! BE BACK IN A SNAP!

WHAT IS ALL OF THIS? YOU SURE DO HAVE A LOT OF PIECES.

THESE ARE INGREDIENTS FOR FAIRY DUST!

OUR RECIPE USES BITS AND BOBS OF EVERYTHING IN THE WOODS!

WE HAVE EVERYTHING WE NEED!

NOW IT'S TIME TO COOK!

OUR SECRET SPOT ISN'T TOO FAR FROM HERE.
THE NEXT PART IS EASY!

WE'LL PUT EVERYTHING INTO YOUR BASKET, NOW. YOU MIGHT WANT TO STAND UP!

THAT DOESN'T SOUND TOO HARD. I'M READY!
PAF!
POOF!

PWOF

WOW!
HOW DID THIS GET HEAVIER?!

EXCUSE ME, MISS? WE HAVE ONE MORE FAVOR TO ASK.

WOULD YOU PLEASE FOLLOW US EXACTLY?
AND VERY CAREFULLY!

OUR COOKING SPOT IS HIDDEN IN THE WOODS!
WE'LL SHOW YOU HOW TO FIND IT.

I'LL BE CAREFUL. LEAD THE WAY!

Zip!

DON'T DROP ANYTHING AS YOU FOLLOW US!

PLEASE KEEP UP!
IT'S NOT VERY FAR, BUT WE HAVE TO GO QUICKLY!

YOU'RE DOING GREAT!

WE'RE ALMOST THERE!

YOU CAN SET IT DOWN HERE, PLEASE!

IT LOOKS LIKE WE HAVE EVERYTHING!

AND YOU DIDN'T LOSE EVEN ONE TINY THING!

HOORAY! WE DID IT! AND IT'S ALL THANKS TO YOU!
YOU REALLY HELPED US OUT!

THANKS AGAIN FOR THE HELP!

WE'RE SORRY YOU CAN'T STAY TO SEE HOW IT'S DONE.
IT'S A SUPER SPECIAL SECRET RECIPE!
PIP!
PIP!
PIP!

THAT'S OKAY. I HAVE THINGS TO DO BACK IN THE ORCHARD.

GOOD LUCK WITH YOUR DUST!

GOODBYE!
TAKE CARE!

OH DEAR.
WHICH WAY DID I COME FROM?

WATCH OUT! THERE'S A BIG PUDDLE OVER THERE!

THISTLE!
OH, I'M GLAD TO SEE YOU. DID YOU FINISH YOUR NAP?

I DID! SO I DECIDED TO CATCH UP AND WALK BACK WITH YOU.

THERE'S A PATH NEARBY. I'LL SHOW YOU THE WAY!

I KNEW FAIRIES HID THINGS IN THE WOODS...
... BUT I DIDN'T THINK IT WOULD BE SO MUCH WORK TO FIND A SPECIAL SPOT!

YOU KNOW, WE LOSE THINGS IN THE WOODS SOMETIMES.

WHAT? LIKE LOSING SOCKS IN THE WASH?
SOMETHING LIKE THAT!

CHAPTER 4

PLUCK!

CHOMP

OH! IT'S SWEET!

THIS SHOULD DO THE TRICK.
JUST A LITTLE SOMETHING SPECIAL!

OF COURSE, MY BASKET WON'T BE AS GOOD AS CLEMENTINE'S ENTRY.
HER ORANGES ARE ALWAYS SO PERFECT!

CLEMETINE IS SO PARTICULAR AND CAREFUL WITH HER WORK.
I BET HER ENTRY WILL BE PERFECT, TOO!

IF ONLY I HAD BEEN BRAVE ENOUGH TO TALK TO HER BEFORE!

MAYBE WE COULD HAVE SWAPPED SECRETS.

POOF!

MAYBE I CAN JUST TALK TO CLEMENTINE AT THE FAIR.
YEAH. I'LL DO THAT.

THESE RIBBONS LOOK NICE! IS SOMEONE HAVING A PARTY?

HUH?!
THOSE RIBBONS ARE COMING FROM MY ROOM???

AH!

HELLO, CALLAWAY!

THISTLE! WHAT ARE YOU UP TO?
THERE ARE RIBBONS EVERYWHERE!

SORRY, I GOT CARRIED AWAY.
I THOUGHT I COULD USE A LITTLE MAGIC FOR MY SECRET PROJECT--

BUT IT TURNED INTO A LOT!

AW. LET ME HELP YOU.

WOW, LOOK AT THIS!

FROM UP HERE, IT LOOKS LIKE A REAL PARTY!

MY ROOM, ON THE OTHER HAND...

SORRY ABOUT THAT. I'LL CLEAN UP!

YOU START HERE, AND I'LL FIND THE OTHER END.
RIGHTO!

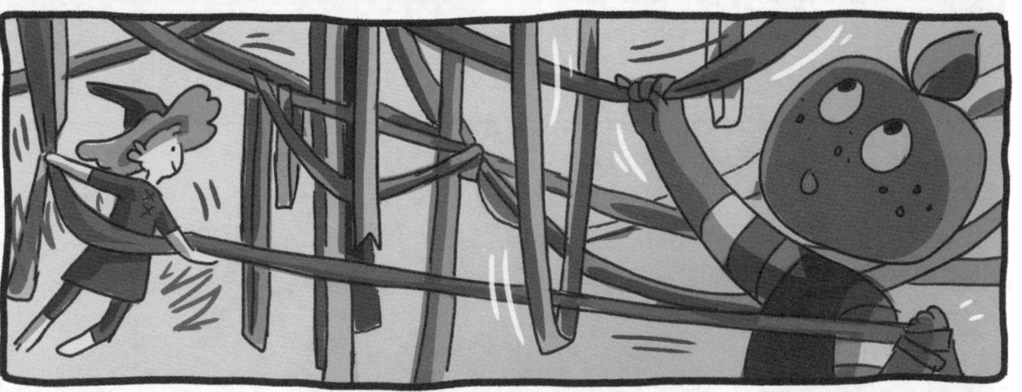

THAT'S A LOT OF RIBBON!

THERE'S STILL MORE UP HERE!

NOW WHAT DO WE DO?
I'LL SHOW YOU!

AW, THISTLE! YOUR BOWS ARE VERY PRETTY!

YOU THINK SO? YOU CAN MAKE ALL KINDS OF SHAPES, EVEN FROM A SMALL PIECE.

BUT WHAT ARE THEY FOR? YOUR SECRET PROJECT, OF COURSE--

OH! THESE ARE PRIZE RIBBONS!
YOU'RE HELPING WITH THE FAIR COMPETITION, AREN'T YOU?

GOOD GUESSER! THEY'RE NOT QUITE PRIZES, YET.

OOOOH!
THEY NEED BADGES!

AFTER THIS, MY SECRET PROJECT WILL BE FINISHED!

1

ARE THESE A SECRET FROM THE OTHER FAIRIES, TOO?
KIND OF. WHEN THE FAIRIES PUT ON AN EVENT LIKE THIS, WE TAKE TURNS DOING DIFFERENT JOBS.
I USUALLY HELP CLEAN UP, BUT THIS YEAR I WANTED TO DO SOMETHING EXTRA SPECIAL.

MAYOR MINT LET ME MAKE THE PRIZE RIBBONS THIS YEAR!
BUT THE OTHER FAIRIES DOUBTED I WAS UP TO THE TASK...

SOME OF THEM STARTED HELPING ME THINK OF WHAT TO DO. OH, THEY WERE WORRIED!

THEY EVEN CALLED ME LAZY, BECAUSE I DIDN'T WANT TO FOLLOW THEIR RULES.

THEY JUST KEPT NAGGING AT ME TO DO IT THIS WAY, OR DO IT THAT WAY.
I COULDN'T CONCENTRATE!

I STILL CARE ABOUT DOING A GOOD JOB! I JUST COULDN'T DO IT WITH THEIR HELP.
THAT'S WHY I NEEDED TO FIND A SECRET PLACE TO WORK.

I'M READY TO SHOW OFF WHAT I'VE MADE NOW.
GOOD THING TOO, SINCE THE CONTEST STARTS TOMORROW.

IS IT TOMORROW ALREADY? I NEARLY FORGOT!

SURE ENOUGH! I EVEN CHECKED OFF A DAY THIS MORNING!

WHAT'S THIS? NO WIGGLES OR JIGGLES?

WOW! NOT ONE.

THISTLE, YOU'VE HELPED WITH MY PROBLEM, TOO. I THINK I'VE FIGURED IT OUT...
I DON'T LIKE BEING IN THE SPOTLIGHT!

I DO LIKE HELPING, BUT I WORRY TOO MUCH ABOUT WHAT MIGHT HAPPEN.
I KNOW IT'S NOT SO IMPORTANT, BUT I STILL THINK A LOT ABOUT WHAT OTHER PEOPLE THINK.

THAT'S WHAT MAKES ME WIGGLE AND SHAKE AND LOSE MY HEAD.

I THINK I NEED TO FIND SOME WAY TO HELP BEHIND THE SCENES.

I CAN HELP YOU WITH THAT TOO!

BUT FIRST, I NEED ONE MORE FAVOR FROM YOU.

WOULD YOU PLEASE CARRY MY RIBBONS TO THE FAIR TOMORROW?

OF COURSE I WOULD!

IN FACT, I HAVE JUST THE THING...

THIS BOX SHOULD HELP KEEP THEM SECRET A LITTLE LONGER!

THAT'S PERFECT!
I HAVE TO GO NOW, BUT I'LL MEET YOU BY THE CONTEST BOOTH IN THE MORNING.

DON'T FORGET MY RIBBONS!

OH, THANK YOU, THISTLE. I WON'T FORGET!
GOODBYE!

CHAPTER 5

YO HO!

I FOUND THESE BASKETS...BUT NO CALLAWAY OR CLEMENTINE!

OH DEAR!
THEY'RE MISSING!

DO YOU THINK SOMETHING HAPPENED?
SHOULD WE WAIT FOR THEM?

OKAY, FRUITS! IT'S TIME FOR US TO GO.

SMITH! CALLAWAY AND CLEMENTINE AREN'T HERE!

MAYBE THEY WENT AHEAD! WE'LL MEET THEM THERE.

WELL, THAT'S THAT, I GUESS.

UH-OH! LOOKS LIKE EVERYONE IS ALREADY HERE!

I DON'T WANT TO MAKE A SCENE...

I'LL JUST FIND ANOTHER WAY!

POP!

WHOOOOP!

AAAAAAAA

OUCH!

EEEEEEEK!

BOP
BOOP
AH!
OOF!
BUMP!

CLEMENTINE???
CALLAWAY!!!

WHAT ARE YOU DOING HERE?
I'M SORRY I BUMPED INTO YOU!

I FORGOT SOMETHING BACK AT THE ORCHARD.
WERE YOU LOOKING FOR ME? I WAS JUST RUNNING LATE.

ALL RIGHT, MISSY! YOU GO FIRST!
NO, YOU!

HAHAHAHAHA AHAHAHAH

PAFF.
OH!

CAN YOU TEACH ME TO DO THAT?

SURE! IT'S A LITTLE HARD AT FIRST, BUT IT GETS EASIER LATER.

PWOP!

THANKS! GOOD AS NEW.

I'M SORRY FOR KNOCKING YOUR HEAD OFF!
I HAVE A SPECIAL JOB TODAY. I WAS IN A HURRY!

IT WASN'T YOUR FAULT.
I WAS TOO NERVOUS TO ENTER THE FAIR AFTER ALL, AND I LOST MY HEAD WHILE DECIDING WHAT TO DO.

I WAS HIDING UNTIL THE FAIR WAS OVER.
THAT SEEMED EASIER THAN EXPLAINING MYSELF.
OH, CLEMENTINE!

DON'T WORRY! I'VE BEEN NERVOUS THIS WEEK, TOO.

YOU PROBABLY NOTICED I HAVEN'T BEEN AROUND AS MUCH LATELY.

NO WAY! I OUGHT YOU WERE JUST BUSY WITH YOUR APPLES.
WELL, I WAS! SORT OF...

I TRIED TO STAY BUSY SO I WOULDN'T LOSE MY HEAD.
BUT I ONLY DECIDED WHAT TO DO ABOUT MY WORRIES YESTERDAY.

I DIDN'T WANT TO MISS OUT ON ALL THE FUN, ESPECIALLY SINCE EVERYONE ELSE WAS SO EXCITED!

BUT I WASN'T VERY EXCITED TO ENTER THE CONTEST EITHER...
SO I'M GOING TO TRY SOMETHING DIFFERENT.

SOMETHING DIFFERENT? LIKE WHAT?

COME WITH ME AND I'LL SHOW YOU.

HELLO, HELLO! YOU'RE RIGHT ON TIME.

AND WHO'S THIS?
THIS IS CLEMENTINE!
SHE'S FEELING A LITTLE SHY TODAY, BUT SHE'S A GREAT HELPER, TOO.

HI THERE! I'M GLAD YOU'RE HERE!

DID YOU BRING MY SURPRISE, CALLAWAY?

OF COURSE I DID!

NOW COME IN QUIETLY. WE'RE JUST HAVING A MEETING BEFORE WE GET STARTED.
I KNEW YOU WOULDN'T LET ME DOWN.

EVERYONE! HELLO!
THANKS TO YOUR HARD WORK, THIS YEAR'S CONTEST IS ABOUT TO BEGIN!

BLUEBELL, YOU'VE TRAINED YOUR TRICKS TO BE SO TALENTED AND CUTE.

THE KIDS WILL LOVE THEM ALL!

WILLOW AND LILY!
YOU'VE WORKED SO HARD ON YOUR SPARKLING FAIRY DUST.

THESE BOTTLES WILL BRING DELIGHT, I'M SURE!

AND HERE'S THISTLE!
DID YOU BRING YOUR RIBBONS IN THAT BOX?

THAT'S RIGHT, MAYOR MINT!

YOU CAN'T HAVE A CONTEST WITHOUT PRIZE RIBBONS!
AAAAH!
OOOOOH!
WOW!

OH, THISTLE, THESE ARE BEAUTIFUL!
THIS ONE MATCHES MY TRICKS!

GOOD WORK, THISTLE! THE CRAFTSMANSHIP IS WONDERFUL!

HE MADE THEM ALL BY HAND, WITHOUT MAGIC!

NO MAGIC?!

HEY, THISTLE! WHY DID YOU KEEP THESE SECRET?
YOU SHOULD HAVE TOLD US YOU WERE WORKING SO HARD!

AW, WILLOW. WOULD YOU HAVE BELIEVED ME?

OKAY, I'LL WORK ON THAT. FRIENDS?

YOU BET!

ALL RIGHT, EVERYONE. THE EVENT WILL BE STARTING SOON!
TO YOUR STATIONS!

THANKS FOR WAITING, GIRLS!
WOULD YOU COME THIS WAY, PLEASE? I'LL SHOW YOU WHAT WE'RE UP TO.

AS YOU CAN SEE, WE HAVE LOTS OF TABLES AND SHELVES.
SOME OF MY FRIENDS ARE VERY GOOD AT ORGANIZING DISPLAYS!

AT THIS TABLE, WE COLLECT THE ENTRIES.

THEN WE SORT THINGS INTO CATEGORIES FOR JUDGING!

JAMS AND JELLIES ARE OVER HERE!

AND PLATES FOR TASTING ARE OVER HERE!

THE VARIETY IS REALLY QUITE SOMETHING!

SOME OF OUR ENTRIES ARE JUDGED ON FLAVOR.

HOT PEPPERS ARE A POPULAR CATEGORY THIS YEAR!

"LIVING FOOD" IS A NEAT CATEGORY, TOO.

HERE'S A GROUP GARDEN DISPLAY THAT LOOKS QUITE NICE.

AND HERE'S A SPECIAL SHELF FOR "BEST IN SHOW"!

WE EVEN HAVE A SPOT FOR WORKS OF ART!

WELL, THAT JUST ABOUT COVERS IT!

WHAT DID YOU THINK?
DID YOU SEE ANYTHING YOU LIKED?

IT WASN'T SO BAD!
IT'S NOT WHAT I IMAGINED AT ALL!

THERE YOU ARE!!!

CALLA! WHERE DID YOU GO? AND CLEMENTINE TOO!

WE LOOKED FOR YOU EARLIER! WHERE DID YOU GO?

THAT'S A LONG STORY. I'LL TELL YOU LATER!

I HOPE YOU'RE NOT UPSET AT US FOR BEING SHY.
WE DIDN'T FEEL LIKE ENTERING THE CONTEST AFTER ALL.

UPSET? NO WAY!

SORRY IF WE GOT CARRIED AWAY ABOUT THE CONTEST.
WE'RE GLAD YOU FOUND SOMETHING SPECIAL TO DO FOR THE FAIR ANYWAY.

CALLAWAY! AND CLEMENTINE!
I'M SO EXCITED TO SEE YOU!

NICE JOB ON YOUR ENTRIES THIS YEAR!
"HONORABLE MENTIONS" FOR BOTH OF YOU!
I'LL HAVE TO THINK OF SOMETHING REALLY SPECIAL IF I WANT TO WIN A PRIZE NEXT TIME.

HUH?!

CALLAWAY, WE KNOW YOU'VE BEEN BUSY HELPING ALL THE OTHER KIDS...

BUT YOU FORGOT TO ENTER YOUR OWN FRUIT IN THE CONTEST, SILLY!

SO WE ENTERED IT FOR YOU.
CONGRATULATIONS!

HOW ABOUT WE GO SEE THE REST OF THE FAIR NOW?
YEAH! THERE'S LOTS OF TASTY FOOD TO TRY!

CHAPTER 6

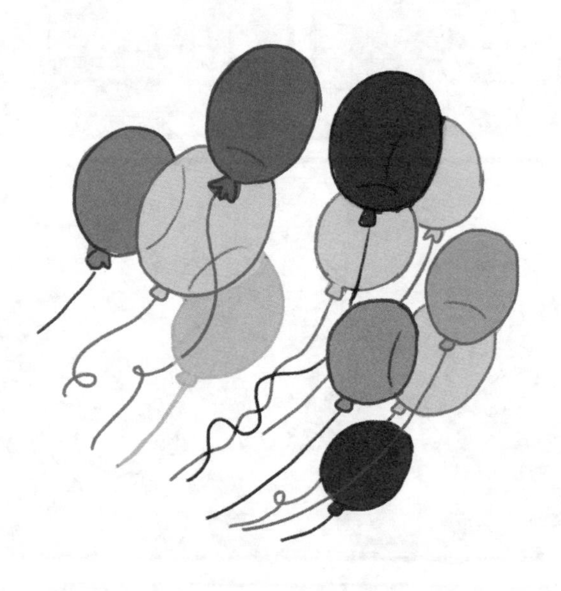

EXIT

Y'KNOW WHAT I HEARD?
THEY'RE PUTTING ON ANOTHER CONTEST NEXT YEAR!

ARE THEY REALLY?
OH BOY! I KNOW JUST WHAT TO MAKE!

HRMPH!
I DIDN'T WIN ANYTHING THIS TIME. I THINK I'M DONE WITH CONTESTS.

AW, DON'T BE CRANKY!
I DIDN'T WIN ANYTHING, EITHER. IT WAS STILL FUN TO TRY!

HEY, EVERYONE! LOOK AT THIS!
IT'S A PAMPHLET FOR A TALENT SHOW!

A TALENT SHOW!

I KNOW A GREAT SONG!

I'LL PLAY MY DRUMS!

I KNOW SOME CARD MAGIC!

WE CAN DO CARTWHEELS AND TUMBLING!

MMMM MMM

POP

SNATCH!

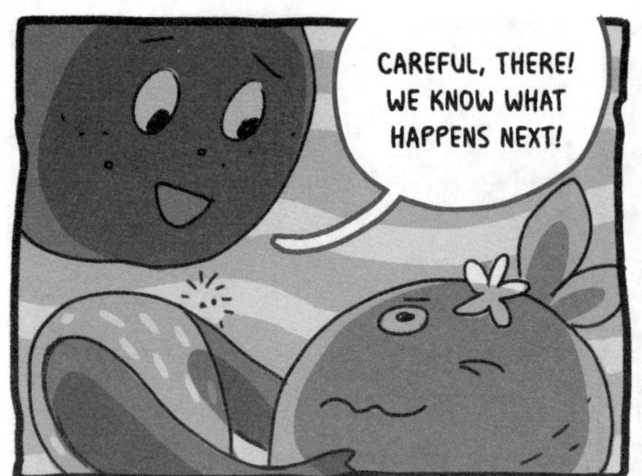
CAREFUL, THERE! WE KNOW WHAT HAPPENS NEXT!

PLUNK!

LET'S TRY TO BE SMART ABOUT THIS...

LOOK HOW EXCITED THEY ARE! IT'S JUST WHAT THEY LIKE.
CLEMENTINE, I THINK I'LL LEAVE THE PERFORMING TO THEM.

AN EVENT LIKE THIS WILL NEED REFRESHMENTS...

WE COULD HELP MAKE SNACKS!

THAT'S GOOD IDEA, ALLAWAY.
YOU KNOW JUST WHAT TO DO!

DID YOU SAY SNACKS???
DESSERTS! WE LOVE DESSERT!!!

CALLA, CAN YOU MAKE APPLESAUCE CAKE?
WITH WARM BUTTER SAUCE?

I LIKE MUFFINS WITH STREUSEL CRUMBS ON TOP!

WHAT ABOUT APPLE ROSES?

I WANT APPLE NUT BREAD!
AND APPLESAUCE!
AND APPLE TURNOVERS!
AND APPLE PIE!

KAETI VANDORN IS AN ILLUSTRATOR AND CARTOONIST WHO LOVES DRAWING COLORFUL LANDSCAPES AND ADORABLE MONSTERS. SHE SPENT HER CHILDHOOD CHASING FIREFLIES IN KANSAS, THEN BEING CHASED BY MOSQUITOES IN ALASKA. SHE HAS RECENTLY MOVED TO VERMONT, WHERE SHE LIVES AT THE TOP OF A BIG GRASSY HILL. SHE STAYS INDOORS MOST OF THE TIME TO AVOID THE TERRIFYING INSECTS OUTDOORS. (ALSO, THAT BIG GUY, SASQUATCH.)

SHE HAS A DEGREE IN ILLUSTRATION FROM THE ACADEMY OF ART UNIVERSITY, WHICH SHE ACHIEVED THROUGH ONLINE CORRESPONDENCE. HER CASUAL INTERESTS LAY IN BOTANY AND HERPETOLOGY; IF SHE WASN'T AN ARTIST (AND NOT SO WARY OF BUGS), SHE WOULD PROBABLY BE A NATURALIST, STUDYING THE BIZARRE AND WONDERFUL CREATURES OF THE WORLD.

AS A FREELANCE ILLUSTRATOR, KAETI HAS THE PLEASURE OF WORKING FROM HOME, WITH AN EVER-CHANGING VARIETY OF TASKS AND THEMES . . . SHE LIKES THIS A LOT! HER DRAWINGS HAVE BEEN FEATURED IN ART BOOKS, INDIE ZINES, AND GALLERY SHOWS ACROSS THE UNITED STATES. MOST RECENTLY, SHE HAS DRAWN COVER ART FOR ALBUMS BY THE MUSICAL ARTIST NANOBII.

KAETI BEGAN SELF-PUBLISHING COMICS ONLINE IN 2014. CRABAPPLE TROUBLE IS KAETI'S FIRST PRINTED BOOK, AND SHE HOPES YOU ENJOY IT VERY MUCH.

t PROTEIDAES.TUMBLR.COM

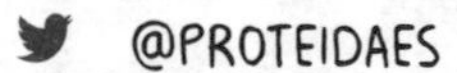

@PROTEIDAES

@PROTEIDAES

CHARACTER CREATION

LET'S DRAW SOME FRUIT AND VEGGIE CHARACTERS! IT'S EASY AND FUN ONCE YOU LEARN TO SEE SIMPLE SHAPES.

CALLAWAY

CRABAPPLES ARE SHAPED LIKE A SQUARE. CAN YOU THINK OF OTHER FRUITS AND VEGGIES THAT HAVE THIS SHAPE?

LET'S DRAW CALLAWAY

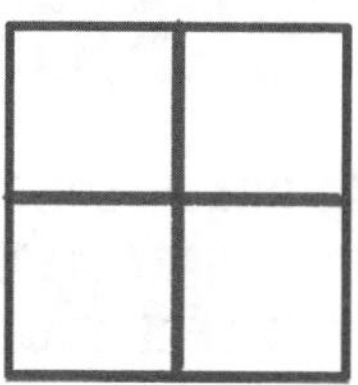

FIRST, LET'S THINK OF A SQUARE. NOW LET'S DIVIDE IT INTO EVEN QUARTERS WITH A CROSS DOWN THE MIDDLE.

2

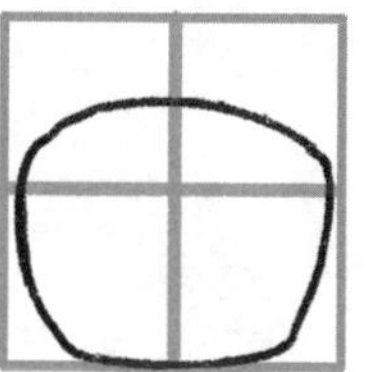

DRAW AN APPLE SHAPE INSIDE THE SQAURE.

3

THE LEAF AND STEM START FROM THE MIDDLE OF THE SQUARE.

4

DRAW THE EYES AND MOUTH ALONG THE MIDDLE LINE.

DON'T FORGET HER FRECKLES! NOW ADD SOME COLOR, AND YOU'RE ALL DONE!

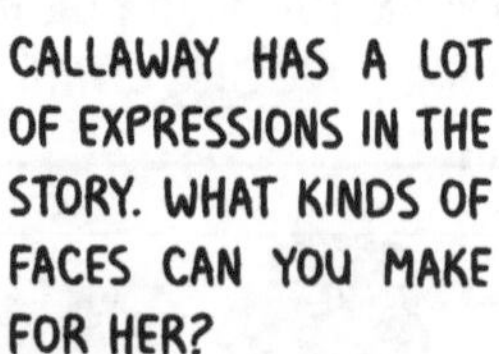

CALLAWAY HAS A LOT OF EXPRESSIONS IN THE STORY. WHAT KINDS OF FACES CAN YOU MAKE FOR HER?

NOW LET'S DRAW A BODY! WE START WITH A SQUARE, LIKE WE MADE BEFORE. STACK THREE OF THESE ON TOP OF EACH OTHER.
1
2
3

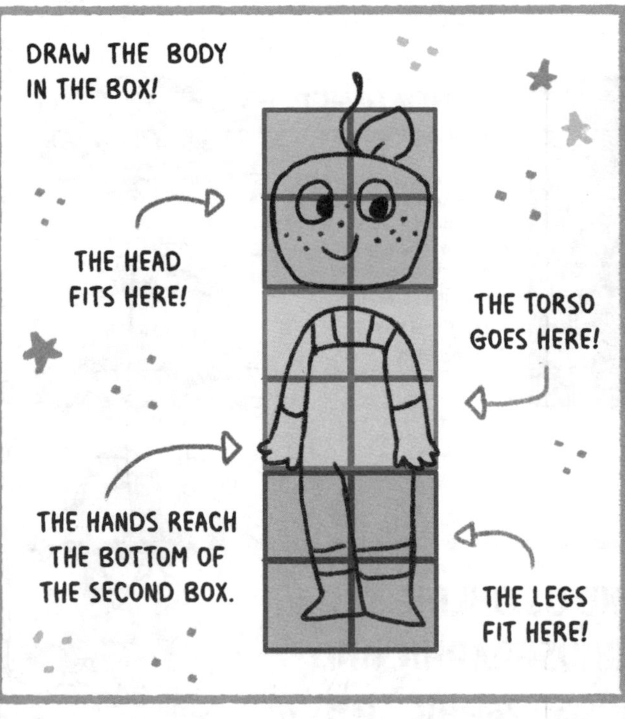
DRAW THE BODY IN THE BOX!
THE HEAD FITS HERE!
THE TORSO GOES HERE!
THE HANDS REACH THE BOTTOM OF THE SECOND BOX.
THE LEGS FIT HERE!

ADD SOME COLOR, AND YOU'RE ALL DONE!

THE SUMMER 2020 LIST

CRABAPPLE TROUBLE

By Kaeti Vandorn

Life isn't easy when you're an apple.

Callaway and Thistle must figure out how to work together—with delicious and magical results.

Young Chapter Book

KERRY AND THE KNIGHT OF THE FOREST

By Andi Watson

Kerry needs to get home!

To get back to his parents, Kerry gets lost in a shortcut. He will have to make tough choices and figure out who to trust—or remain lost in the forest . . . forever.

Middle Grade

STEPPING STONES

By Lucy Knisley

Jen did not want to leave the city.

She did not want to move to a farm.

And Jen definitely did not want to get two new "sisters."

Middle Grade

SUNCATCHER

By Jose Pimienta

Beatriz loves music—more than her school, more than her friends—and she won't let anything stop her from achieving her dreams.

Even if it means losing everything else.

Young Adult

FIND US ONLINE AT @RHKIDSGRAPHIC AND RHKIDSGRAPHIC.COM